The Seven Legged Astronaut

By Lauren Molesworth

A book to inspire young readers into science extend their vocabulary with a bit of quirky humour, while also having a healthy respect to wildlife.

I tell this story not just through my own imagination but also from my upbringing. Being raised by scientist parents and in the great Australian bush, I had many interactions with wildlife. This combination influenced my development into the person I am today and continue to be.

Without approaching the strange (spiders or those different to us) fear will grow where curiosity should have blossomed. Without knowledge (science) to how and why we are here we would become blind to what should be a brighter tomorrow.

Initially I was inspired from Beatrix potter with her watercolours and use of dialect in her stories. I feel I share her humour and hope my style carries a similar presence, but still uniquely my own.

I am not very popular my Instagram is – Laurenthewalkingsiren

I was a paediatric nurse and before that had many dealings with helping sick children.

Contact– lauren.molesworth.candy@gmail.com

On a bright sunny day, a creative huntsman spider excitedly chirps away. "Noak Noak Noak" the sounds of his fangs made in anticipation.

All 7 of his legs work in synchrony, documenting his findings. As the sunlight hits the glass ball, his experiment reveals more questions about the universe.

The spider rubbed his fangs, this time in contemplation before a revelating sound "AaaaaHaaa", sprang out.

This spider of which I speak, his name is Maurice, my friend. He has a bright beautiful orange coat and white polka dots along his legs. With probably not the most flattering of hairdo statements, but who am I to judge. How he came into my life, I shall reveal in another tale. This story however is about Maurice and his quest to explore space.

Even in his sleep Maurice dreams of space.

Do spiders dream? Well, Maurice does and doesn't he ever have such amazing colourful dreams. Propelling through the vacuum of space to new worlds, mapping the stars. Maurice's legs curl up tight giving his alien teddy 'Kale' a big squeeze, while sighing happy content sounds in his sleep.

Sadly, not many other spiders shared his passion for science. Their glazed apathetic glares would often sink Maurice's chirps to a still.

Onwards, Maurice thought. Maurice did not give up and pursued on, hoping one day to find a friend who'd share his enthusiasm for science.

Maurice held lectures on his unsuspecting students. He would patiently wait for the students to quieten down after exhaustion overtakes their entangled body, caught in his sticky webs. Accepting their fate, the lesson proceeds.

Realising the need to capture the audience attention, Maurice moves onto his favourite topic 'Space'.

No one can be disappointed about Kale the alien, or so he thought. Maurice pulls out his beloved puppet.

"Say hello to Kale the alien". Protesting pupils can be heard by their begging groans and moans.

"Eat me, just hurry up and eat me", cried out an infuriated pupil stuck in the back corner of Maurice's lecture room.

Another unsuccessful lecture. With a full stomach and a heavy heart, Maurice's hope dwindles. Elongated fuzzy legs drag his deflated body along the window sill as the cold rain trickles down the glass. The weather matching his bleak outlook of today's events.

Just by chance, Maurice wakes up in the middle of the day and notices a human child reading a science magazine.

All 8 of his eyes widen, intensifying on the contents inside the book.

Planets, Stars, Moons and Nebulas. A new opportunity had presented itself. Maurice chatters his fangs together,

"Noak, Noak". Maurice coerced himself

−NO time to be a coward time to investigate and gather data. After all, what scientist would he be if he stopped at the sight of danger.

Keeping his distance not to be seen by the human.

Maurice hangs dangling dangerously close, but just out of the child's peripheral vision.

The child's eyes transfixed on the book. So, to was Maurice's eyes glued to the pages content. They both read in perfect silence, absorbing, questioning while expanding their minds. Knowledge shared and appreciated between two very different life forms on this round rock flying through space, spinning on a track laid out in star dust.

As the child's day begins, Maurice crawls off to slumber after such a thrilling read. Most spiders are nocturnal after all.

As dusk begins Maurice is eager to find out what the child is up to now. This leads Maurice's investigation to stumble across some unusual metal gear laid out across the bench. Slowly Maurice walks along the cold bench top while rubbing his hairy chin. Intrigued he was, but also confused as to what they could be.

The child dashes past Maurice in a speedy haste. "Hurry its starting, quickly now, quickly" cooed out the older lady of the house.

~I hear the lady is a bit cuckoo upstairs. Although wisdom is her constant companion, when the links align correctly that is~

With everyone settled in the dark lounge room, the television starts. A slow rising instrumental tune begins increasing its tempo as more out of this world images appear on the screen.

 Enthralled, the young child and Maurice scoff down butter popcorn, eyes not daring to look away for a second.

The humans replicated an action seen on the television screen with their hands. Maurice too, copies their hand gestures with his tiny two toed paws.

(That's right, spiders have adorable little paws on the end of each leg.)

Never had Maurice felt like he belonged in something bigger then himself until now. What Maurice is about learn is we all belong together in a great forever expanding, weaving universe. Each and everything is connected like a large tapestry cloth.

No matter how far apart or large the cloth grows. Everything is connected and pulled, shaped, tugged and even influenced by the strings that connect us all.

The old lady turns the television off as the program rolls through the credits. The old lady crooks her head up to look out at the window. The black night sky twinkles back at her beaming eyes. "Its time" She chimes while ushering the child to gather outside the back porch.

The strange metal cylinders that lay previously on the bench had now been set up by the full grown human ready for star gazing. The telescope!

~This equipment uses multiple glass lenses and has been used for about 400years. In many ways, a telescope is a looking glass into what's out there in space. ~

Maurice waited patiently by the porch window for his turn. After the humans took a step back from star gazing, this gave Maurice his moment to take a peak. Maurice snuck daintily up to the telescopes eyepiece before peering in.

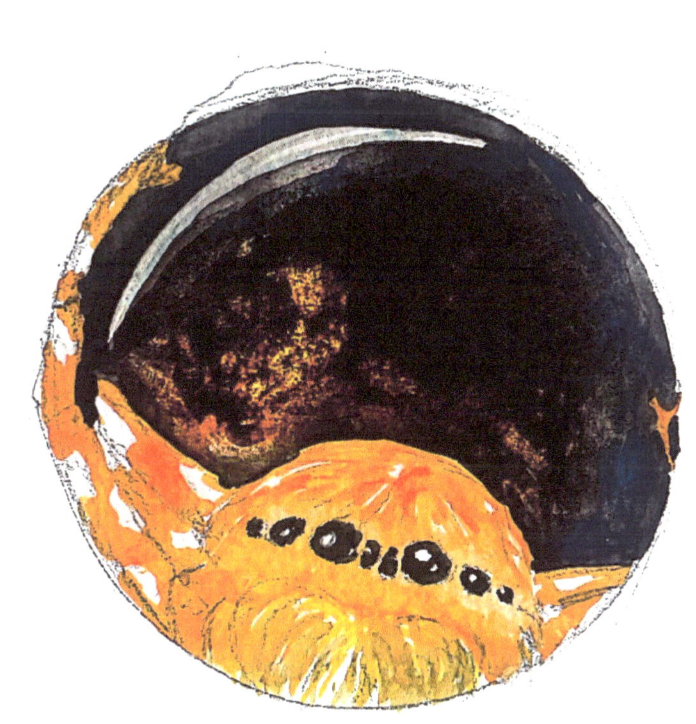

He gulped at the view. *So strange, so peculiar but oddly familiar like our clouds, Maurice thought.*

"Creeek, Thump", dropped the old ladies body into the porch chair. She gathered her thoughts with a slight guttural sound before sharing fascinating facts about space.

"The Andromeda is our neighbouring galaxy almost twice the size of our galaxy. It's so large the galaxy can be seen with the naked eye, although without a telescope it would only appear like another star," stated the old lady.

Part 2

Maurice waits in anticipation for the little human to come back. Hearing the front gate swing open and tapping feet hop along the crunching footpath.

Maurice sails down the window and springs up on the window sill. Waving his multiple legs with excitement needing to be expelled out somewhere as if he had gathered too many positive electrons. He was not short of being a static seven legged hair ball.

"Snip! Snip! Crinkle! and Splat"! Maurice already heavily invested in the child's inquisitive nature into science he could not resist taking a closer look. Placing himself behind a glass jar giving him the perfect viewing point. The child was in the company of another. Not a child but a full-grown human. Both humans where holding colours being bent and split into shapes, then bonded together to form new shapes. Colours swirled in liquid states forming a completely different new colour.

"Aaaaah"! the child screamed upon taking out the paint brush from the water. The sudden sighting of Maurice was a startling fright. What Maurice did not understand was, he had positioned himself behind a glass filled jar which was magnifying his mouth.

~Now in the child's defence. If I were to see a mouth salivating full of sharp hairy fangs with bulging eyes looking right up at me. I'd probably let out a squeal too. Actually, I can say for certainty I would as Maurice gave me many frights early on as we grew accustomed to each other's presence. For one, he got into the habit of pouncing and landing on my head from the banister like my scalp was one giant helipad landing. "Keep your mouth shut and don't look up, when around the designated Maurice bungee plunge", I'd announce too new house guests like a traffic control operator. Sorry, getting side tracked again. Where was I? Oh, got it. Ok now, on with the story. ~

"Do not be afraid of the unknown". The grown human gently ushers the child back to the table. "Fear of what's different will prevent you from growing. Let's take the time to learn from this new guest while giving them respectable space. Observe if they are hostile or are they simply being", Directed the larger human.

"I think the spider is harmless". The child hesitantly gives an answer. At which the Adult responds "nothing is harmless including nothing". This confusing response puzzled the child. With a small acknowledging smile the adult reiterated "if you were a juicy fly, our guest here would most certainly be dangerous".

Maurice bravely stepped into the human's world gazing above. No sudden movements, just a simple acknowledgment of one another. The child revealed her teeth like the larger human. So, to then did Maurice, but this time no one flinched. A successful first contact.

Late at night Maurice waited for the child to fall into a restful sleep. He knew for certain that whatever was happening earlier on the table it had something to do with space. This Maurice had to see.

Spheres of colours easily recognisable as the planets of our solar system dazzled the plains with sparkly glitter and twinkling stars. Maurice slowly walked through soaking all the sensory stimuli in.

Not long into the exploration did Maurice's true-self surface. Scampering about all over the science diorama.

Nothing was holding this mad scientist back, not even gravity nor a bed time.

When Maurice thought the Space exploration had come to an end. A familiar shape caught his eye, hidden behind the Sun revealed a Rocket Ship. The pinnacle of space travel exploration.

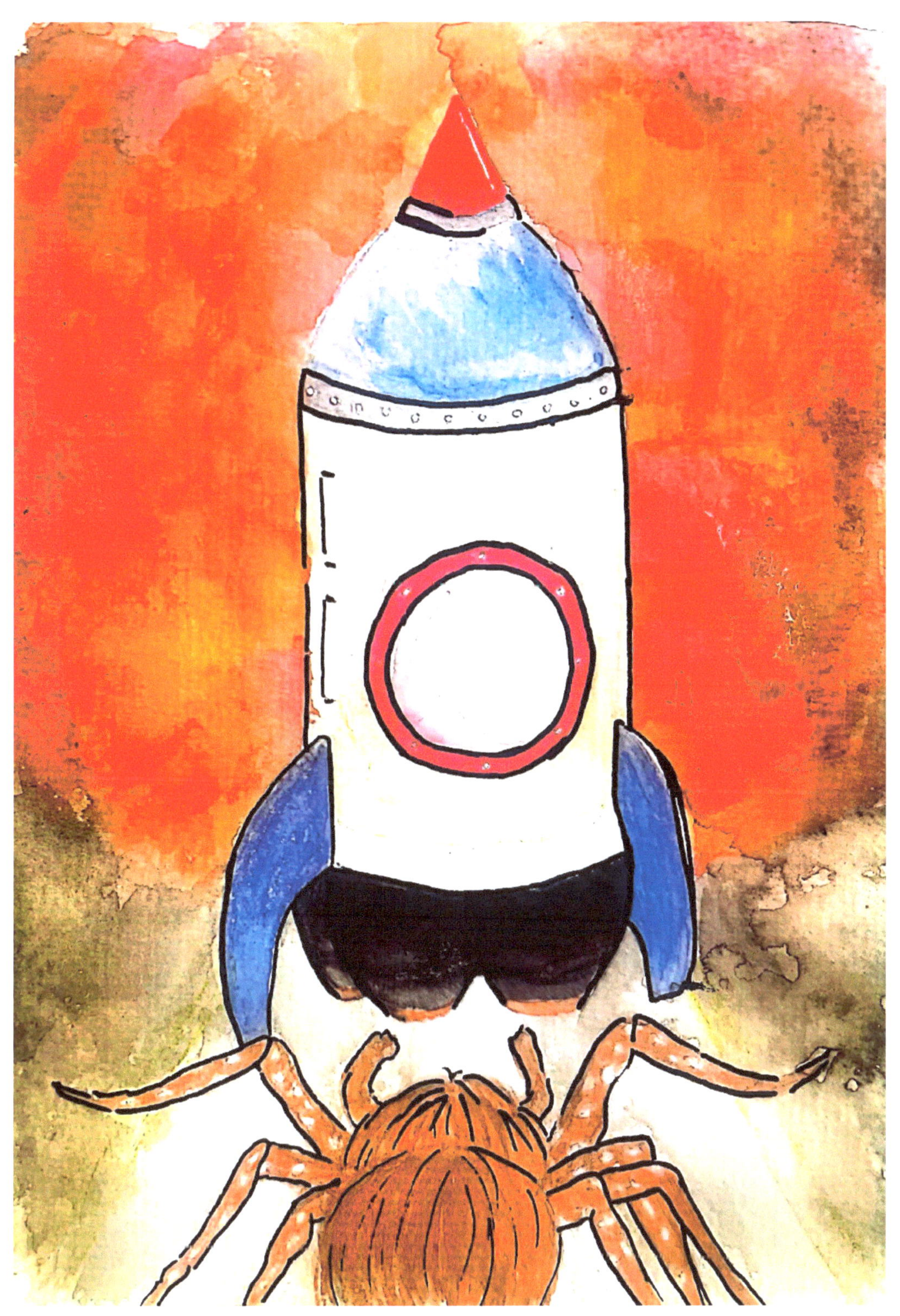

Ecstatic with glee, Maurice threw his front legs into the air while bounding along the table like a spider on a hot plate.

As Maurice crawled up inside the rocket ship, the inside compartments were covered in bright buttons and scanners. No space vessel would be completed without them.

Maurice looks out of the rocket ship window with his leg out stretched reaching to the stars.

Next stop, the unknown

Synopsis

A 7 legged huntsman spider named Maurice is on the pursuit to understand the universe and explore space through the wonder of a child's world. The spiders approach and interaction with the child holds a sense of reality to make the story feel more plausible. While also delving into the spiders perspective. This spider has not come from the fabrication of my imagination entirely. There truly is a 7 legged spider named Maurice living in my house having constant interactions with me. (Almost like having a mini fuzzy shadow.)

Now the reason for his name is simply because his gorgeous face reminds me of an orangutan. The space theme because I love space.

So slap those two together and we have a classic favourite movie franchise. "The Planet Of The Apes". I don't think however turning my illustration novel into a time paradox of spiders enslaving humans and vice versa would work out very well. Oh well c'est la vie I can always try Netflix.

 My intentions ~ are to create multiple small stories with wildlife characters children will often see in their environment. Including my permanent bed n breakfast feathered residents. Mr Gerald Collingwood and his unusual daughter, Ms Maggie Collingwood.

There's alot behind this tale, it's almost hard to write down as being believable but if you need proof I'm sure they wouldn't mind being interviewed.

About myself:

I have always found a good story can start me up on a good day and end on a happy night, just in time for dreaming. Growing up with health issues and an unstable beginning required me to look for escapism, which helped me see my reality in a different light. Giving me whimsical connections to nature and all the creatures I had around me in my childhood garden "the great Australian bush". A friend can always be found, you just have to be open to the possibility of how many eyes or legs a friend can have.

In Honour Of Cotton

~ my best friend, a wonderful dog~

I've had a long-term dream of creating several children's illustrated stories with animal friends. Showing the importance of our connection an interaction between other species. What has finally made me pursue this endeavour was not a build-up of support but the opposite. A tragedy, my entire support structure and will collapsed when I lost my dog my who was my best friends and baby boy

'Cotton'. In the months of blindness wallowing, making it though each day, I still longed and craved a connection and almost unknowingly sought out friendship within those around me. I truly believe these animals knew my heart was aching. They helped me and continue helping me. Through these stories I am expressing the small rays of joy I still have for life. So, this story is in honour to my world my best friend who had two eyes, a black wet nose and four hairy white legs. His name was Cotton and he was a dog. In loving memory of you and the love you gave me lives on through my work.

By lauren Molesworth

www.ingramcontent.com/pod-product-compliance
Lightning Source LLC
Chambersburg PA
CBHW041412300726
48978CB00002B/71